D0531929

Dedicated to imaginary animals waiting to be born.

Positive Press/Star Bear Books
P.O. Box 7626
Chico, CA 95927
(800) 256-8582

Published on recycled paper in Hong Kong
First Edition. First Printing

Gilbar, Rhyk (Richard), 1952–
The Night of the Hippo-fly-tamus/Rhyk Gilbar; illustrated by Steve Ferchaud.–1st ed.
32pp., 25.4x20.3 cm

Summary: An outrageous ecology story. Silly, fantastic creatures abound.

ISBN 1-888588-13-6 hc   LC#97-65162
ISBN 1-888588-14-4 pb

The Night
of the
Hippo-fly-tamus

Written by Rhyk Gilbar
Illustrated by Steve Ferchaud

Some interesting creatures
Use their best features
On the beautiful island of Zort.
Without ever a doubt,
Everybody helps out,
Both the tall and the short.

The Shmergus trims trees,
With spines on his knees,
A very exhausting activity.
And though he's so tall,
He can't bend down at all,
'Cause his legs just don't have bendablity.

So, he asks some Twerns
To pick fruit which he burns,
'Cause Shmergus likes to eat sweets.
Up the smoke goes.
Shmergus eats through his nose.
It's strange but that's the way that he eats.

Twerns have feathers for eyelashes
And long snowflake tresses,
The latest style, it's called.
But on days when it's hot,
Happy they're not
Because every ten minutes they're bald.

Luckily, there's Ploobs
Who love to make snowflake hairdos.
But Ploobs also need some good tending.
So a Hippo-fly-tamus flock
Keeps them well-stocked
With hard-to-get special grape pudding.

With their favorite meal
Under their belts,
The Ploobs re-flake the Twerns
Every time their hair melts.

You'd think that a Snubble
Would live in a bubble
Because that would make a good rhyme.
But Snubbles HATE bubbles.
They make nothing but grumbles,
Even though they make them from their behind.

But the Jub LOVES the bubbles
From the behinds of Snubbles
Gathering them is his delight.
The Ploobs take Jub bundles
And use them for candles
So they can keep on hairstyling at night.

There was a terrible fright
When the Hippo-fly-tamus flight
was cancelled due to bad weather.
And the dear little Ploobs
Had to do without food
So they nibbled on Twern eyelash feathers.

When the Twerns awoke in the morning,
They knew without warning
That something just wasn't right:
Their hair lay in puddles,
Their brains a bit muddled,
And their eyelids unusually light.

With a guilty, fake smile
The Ploobs ran a mile
Away from the naked eyed Twerns.
The Twerns, though quite mad,
Touched their bald heads and were sad
And begged for the Ploobs to return.

The eyelash feathers weren't filling
And without their grape pudding
The Ploobs got weak in the knees.
The weak and sad Ploobs
Refused to eat fruit
And even rare Twernberry seeds.

The Twerns forgot about Shmergus
Which made him quite nervous
And he started to shake in the knees.
And because of his spikes
And lack of fruit which he likes
He chopped down half of the trees.

So the Jub made a bubble bouquet
To send far away
To the land where the grape pudding grew.
The bubbles were tied with great care by the Jub
But when they got there, they were all mixed up.
What they spelled, nobody knew.

MEND SORE DINGDUP?
PUG SNORED MID END?
IGNORE DENSE DUMP?

SEND MORE PUDDING!

The Hippo-fly-tamus took flight,
When they got the letters right
To the place where the Gnax make the puddin
They filled up their buckets
And flew off like rockets
To feed the hungry, sad Ploobs.

It rained and it hailed.

It snowed and it snailed.

The brave Hippos never did stop.

They lit Snubble bubbles,

To save them some troubles

And got there without spilling a drop.

The Ploobs now well-fed
To work they now sped
A special Twern hairdo delight.
To thank the Hippos
They asked them to pose
For their dangerous mission that night.

The Snubble felt proud
And made bubbles, quite loud
And joined in the mood of the party.
But nobody dared,
Or maybe nobody cared
That it started to smell a bit farty.

The Snubble even smiled,
When the Hippos went wild,
Doing some tricks in the air.

The Ploobs sang and danced,
Put snowballs in Jub pants,
Who giggled without seeming to care.

So everyone does their part
With plenty of heart
This makes them happy inside.
So I hope that you see,
We need you, we need me.
Life's great with friends by your side.

Inside your tv live Vee and live Vit.
They suck out your brains while you sit there and sit.
While you are just staring at one of your shows,
They sneak from behind and suck your brains
through your toes.
Yes, they suck out your brains and
your own thoughts they do flee.
Then Vee tells them to Vit, and
Vit tells them to Vee.
Yes, they enjoy your great stories
at night there inside.
Your own stories try to hold on,
but there's nowhere to hide.
They're so much better
than those factory
made tales
But they don't do
very much for
cereal sales.

VEE

VIT

So tell your own stories to Mom before
you forget them.
And don't you let Vee or Vit ever get
at them.
If you have to watch your favorite show,
Keep one eye on the tube but keep one on your toes.